For Rosa
and her fairy godmother,
Naomi

Copyright © 1997 by Bob Graham

All rights reserved.

First U.S. edition 1997

Library of Congress Cataloging-in-Publication Data

Graham, Bob, date.
Queenie, one of the family / Bob Graham.—1st U.S. ed.
Summary: Caitlin and her parents rescue a hen from a lake,
name her, and take her home with them, but even after they return
her to the farm where she lived, her presence is still felt in Caitlin's family.
ISBN 0-7636-0359-7
[1. Chickens—Fiction. 2 Family life—Fiction.]
PZ7.G751667Qu   1997
[E]—dc21   96-52757

10 9 8 7 6 5 4 3 2

Printed in Hong Kong

This book was typeset in Garamond Book Educational.
The pictures were done in watercolor and ink.

Candlewick Press
2067 Massachusetts Avenue
Cambridge, Massachusetts 02140

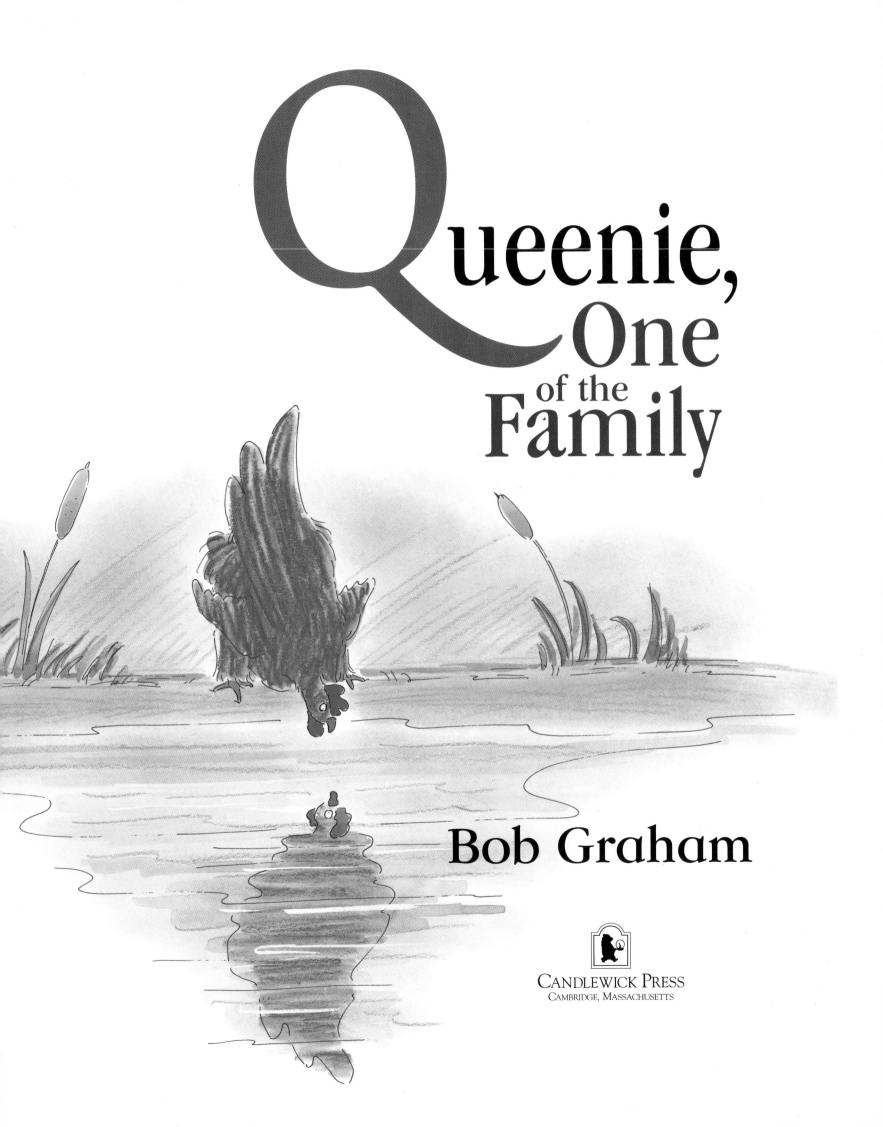

Queenie, One of the Family

Bob Graham

CANDLEWICK PRESS
CAMBRIDGE, MASSACHUSETTS

"Look!" said Caitlin's dad.
"What is it?" asked Caitlin's mom.
"It's a hen in the lake,"
 replied Dad, and he
 did not hesitate.

Off came his shoes, off came his socks,

off came his hat, off came Caitlin!

Caitlin's dad knew that the hen was in trouble.
Big trouble!

"She's a bantam," said Mom.

"Wrap her up warm," said Dad.

"What's your name? Hatty? Tessa? Molly?" said Mom. "No, Queenie! I think you're a Queenie!"

BRUNO lives here

That might have been the end of the story . . . but it wasn't!

Queenie was soon
very much at home
in Bruno's basket.

And in time, Queenie saw
Caitlin's first steps—
   one,
      two,
         three.
Queenie had become one
of the family.

But Caitlin's mom knew
that Queenie had
a home of
her own.

"I think she lives on the farm over the hill from the lake,"
said Mom. So Mom and Dad and Caitlin
and Bruno set off for the farm.

Mom was right.
This was Queenie's home.

Caitlin, her mom and dad, and Bruno the dog went home with milk and cheese and fresh eggs.

And Bruno got his basket back.

That might have been the end of the story . . . but it wasn't!

The next morning,
Queenie got up before the sun.

She flew over the fence, and ran along the path
and past the churchyard.

She went around the lake

and through the woods . . .

over the road,

across the park . . .

and down the street to Caitlin's house.

And in Bruno's basket,
Queenie laid a single perfect egg.

It was Caitlin who found the egg that morning.
And the next morning. And the next.

Every morning Queenie made her journey from the
farm to Caitlin's house and back,

leaving the gift of a small brown egg.

Only once did they spy on Queenie laying
her egg, and never again.

"It didn't seem right," said Mom. "It seemed . . ."
"Private," said Dad.

And so the weeks turned to months.

There were
changes in
Caitlin's house.

There was a new
baby in the family.

The story might have
ended right there . . .
but it didn't!

After the new baby came home,
Caitlin forgot to collect Queenie's eggs.

Bruno reclaimed his basket

and Queenie never returned.

Bruno hatched the eggs. . . .

CHICKS!

"Those chicks need their mother," said Mom.
So they all went back to the farm.

"There's Queenie!"
said Caitlin.

Caitlin's mom and dad and the new baby
went home with bread and milk and cheese.
And guess what Caitlin brought home!

Bruno made room for yet
another addition to the family!
One day the chick will be full grown and
may see Caitlin's brother take his first steps.

But that's another story.